Dear Parents:

Congratulations! Your child is taking the first steps on an exciting journey. The destination? Independent reading!

STEP INTO READING® will help your child get there. The program offers five steps to reading success. Each step includes fun stories and colorful art or photographs. In addition to original fiction and books with favorite characters, there are Step into Reading Non-Fiction Readers, Phonics Readers and Boxed Sets, Sticker Readers, and Comic Readers—a complete literacy program with something to interest every child.

Learning to Read, Step by Step!

Ready to Read   Preschool–Kindergarten
• big type and easy words • rhyme and rhythm • picture clues
For children who know the alphabet and are eager to begin reading.

Reading with Help   Preschool–Grade 1
• basic vocabulary • short sentences • simple stories
For children who recognize familiar words and sound out new words with help.

Reading on Your Own   Grades 1–3
• engaging characters • easy-to-follow plots • popular topics
For children who are ready to read on their own.

Reading Paragraphs   Grades 2–3
• challenging vocabulary • short paragraphs • exciting stories
For newly independent readers who read simple sentences with confidence.

Ready for Chapters   Grades 2–4
• chapters • longer paragraphs • full-color art
For children who want to take the plunge into chapter books but still like colorful pictures.

STEP INTO READING® is designed to give every child a successful reading experience. The grade levels are only guides; children will progress through the steps at their own speed, developing confidence in their reading.

Remember, a lifetime love of reading starts with a single step!

RHUS39614

 Published in the United States by Random House Children's Books, a division of Penguin Random House LLC, 1745 Broadway, New York, NY 10019, and in Canada by Penguin Random House Canada Limited, Toronto.

Visit us on the Web!
StepIntoReading.com
rhcbooks.com
dckids.kidswb.com

Educators and librarians, for a variety of teaching tools, visit us at RHTeachersLibrarians.com

ISBN 978-1-5247-6864-5 (trade)
ISBN 978-1-5247-6865-2 (lib. bdg.)
ISBN 978-1-5247-6866-9 (ebook)

Printed in the United States of America
10 9 8 7 6 5 4 3 2 1

DC SUPER FRIENDS

FAST AS THE FLASH!

by Christy Webster

illustrated by Erik Doescher

Random House 🏠 New York

Meet The Flash.

He is a super hero.

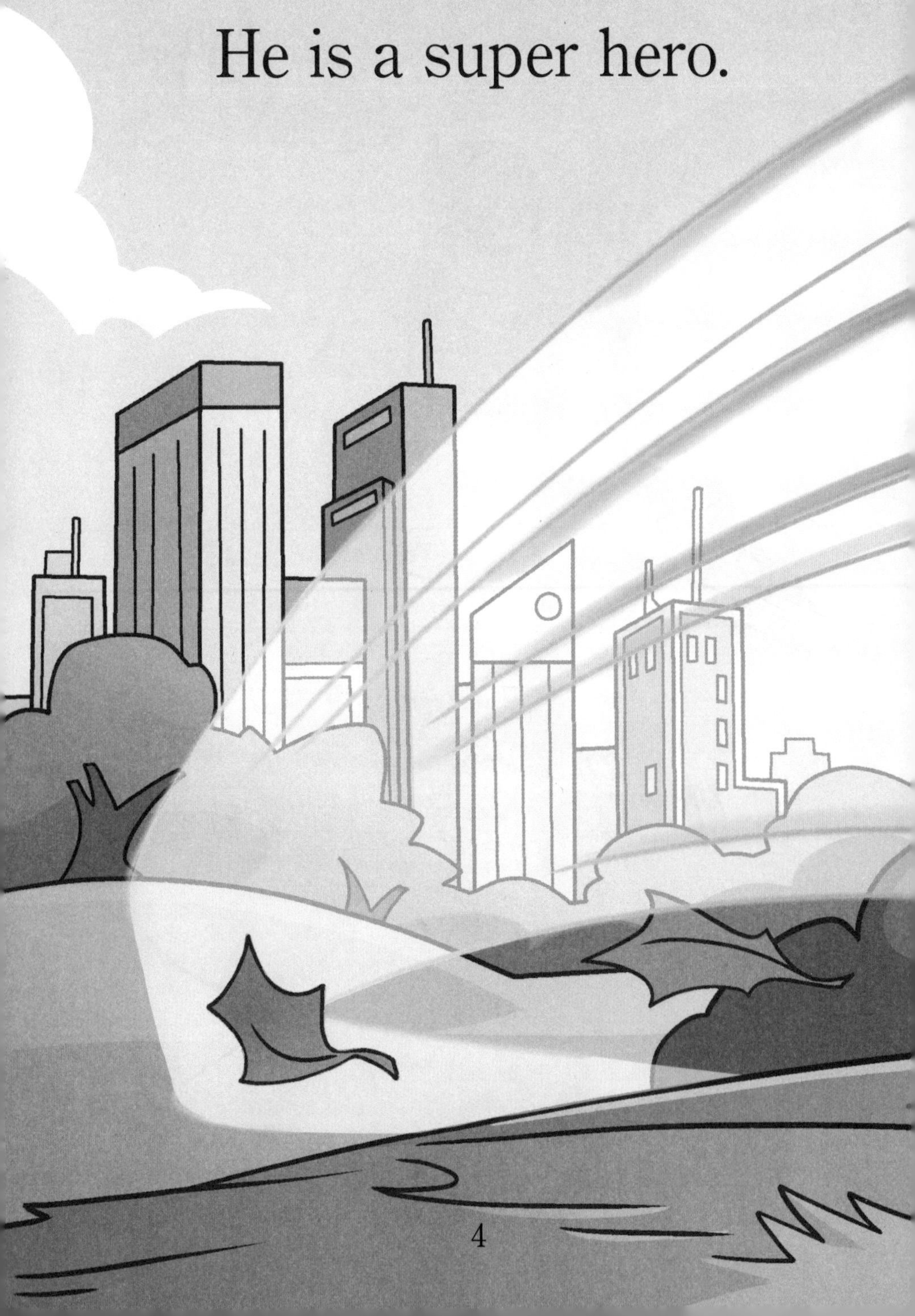

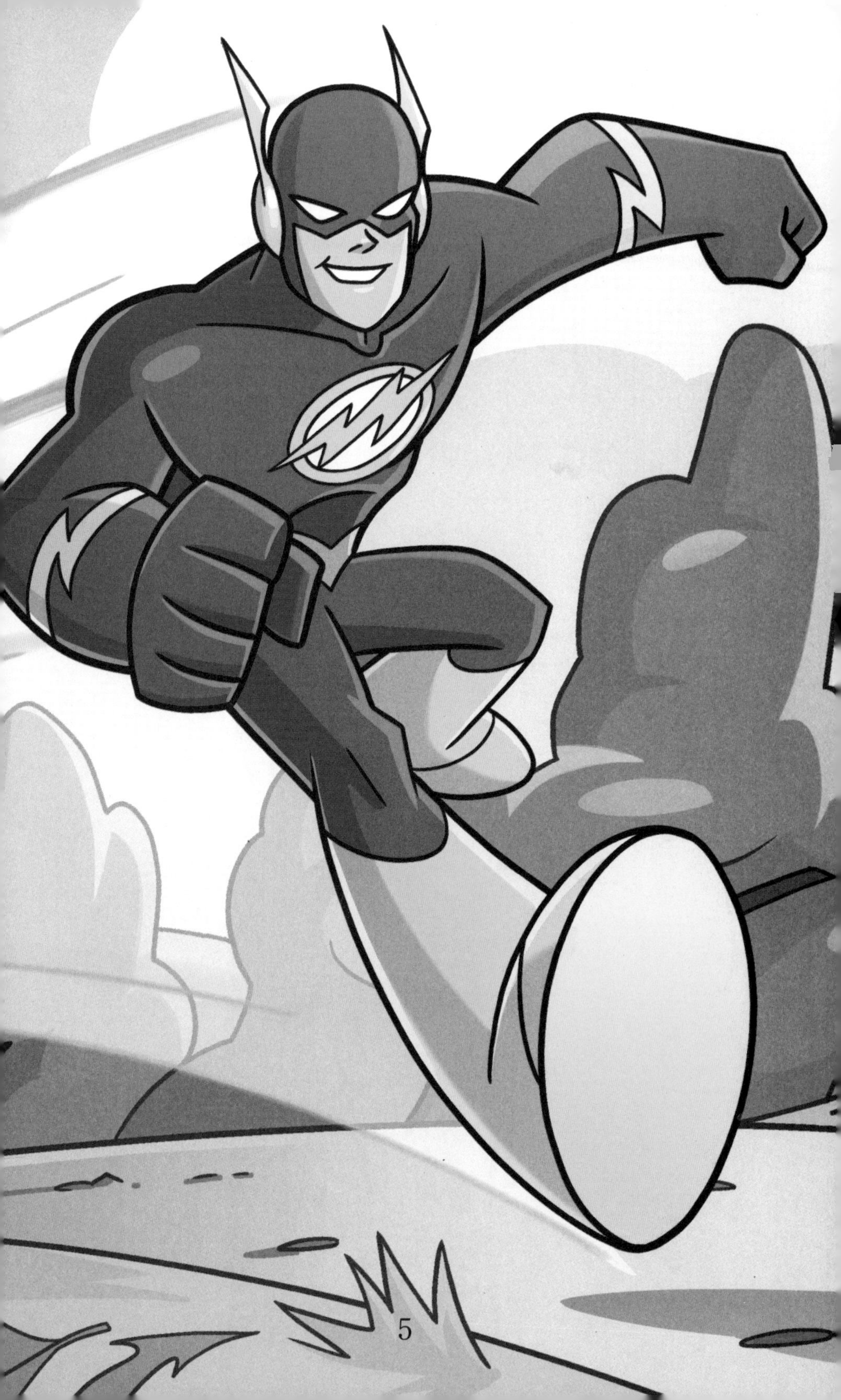

The Flash was
a policeman.
He used science
to solve crimes.

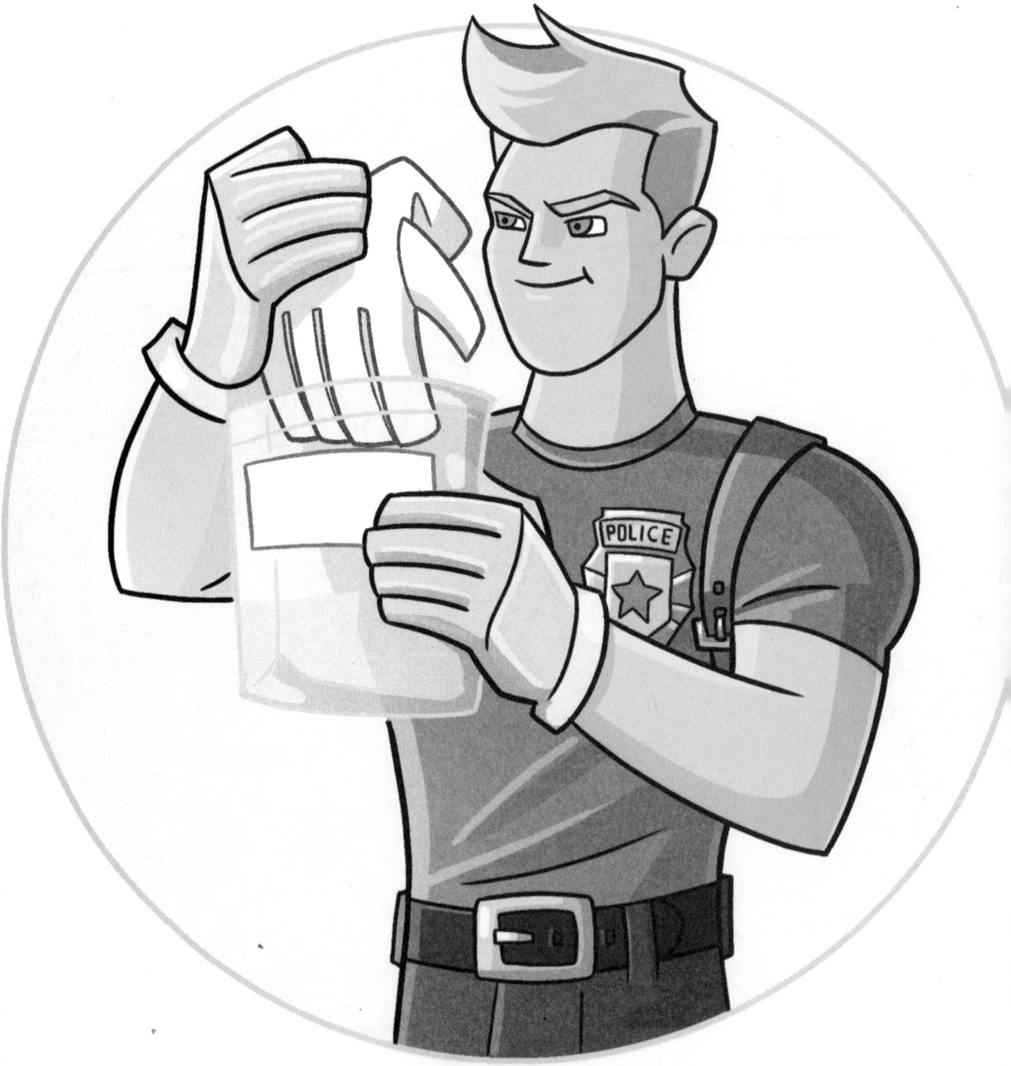
POLICE

A lightning bolt
hit his lab one day.
It smashed bottles.
Something spilled
on him.

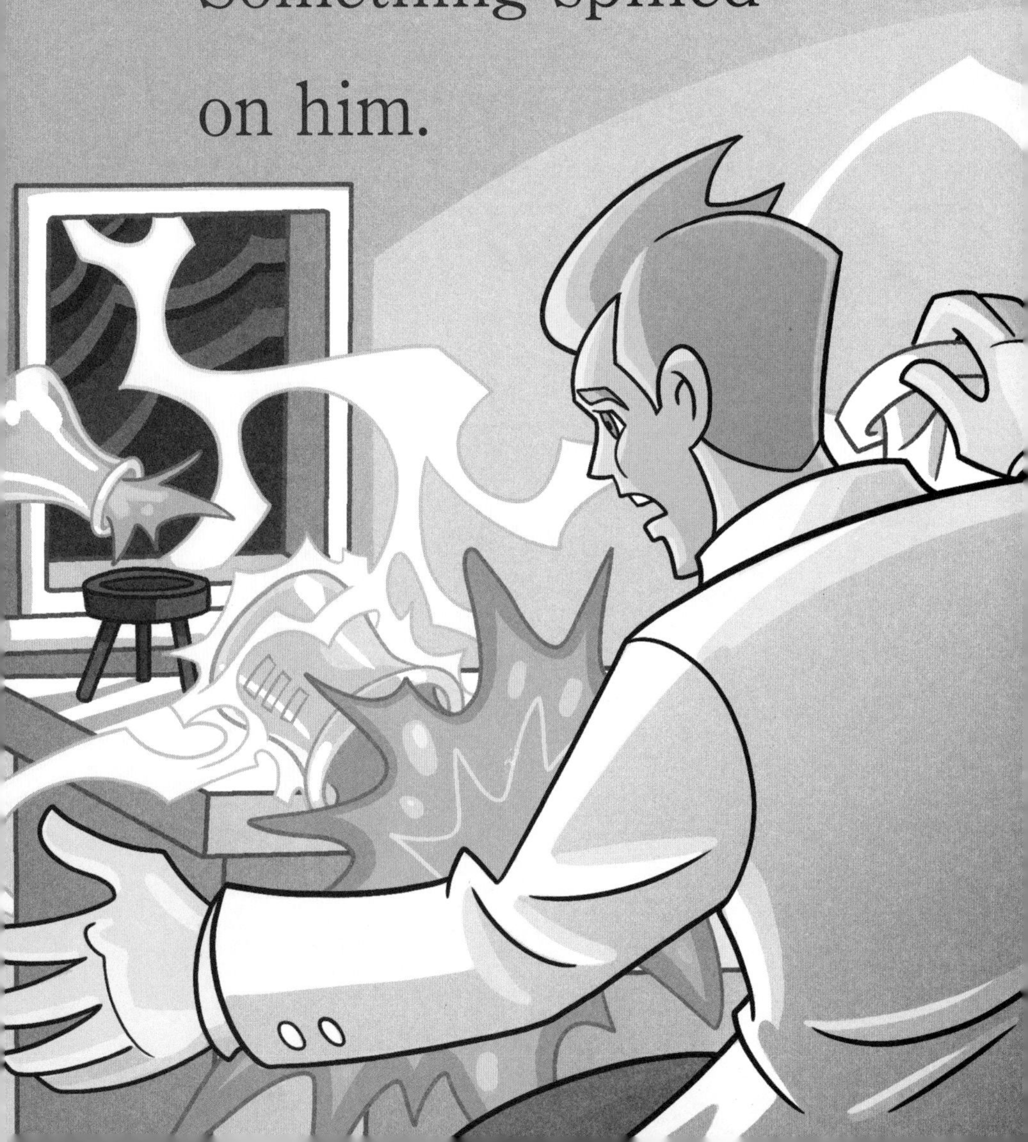

It made him

super-fast.

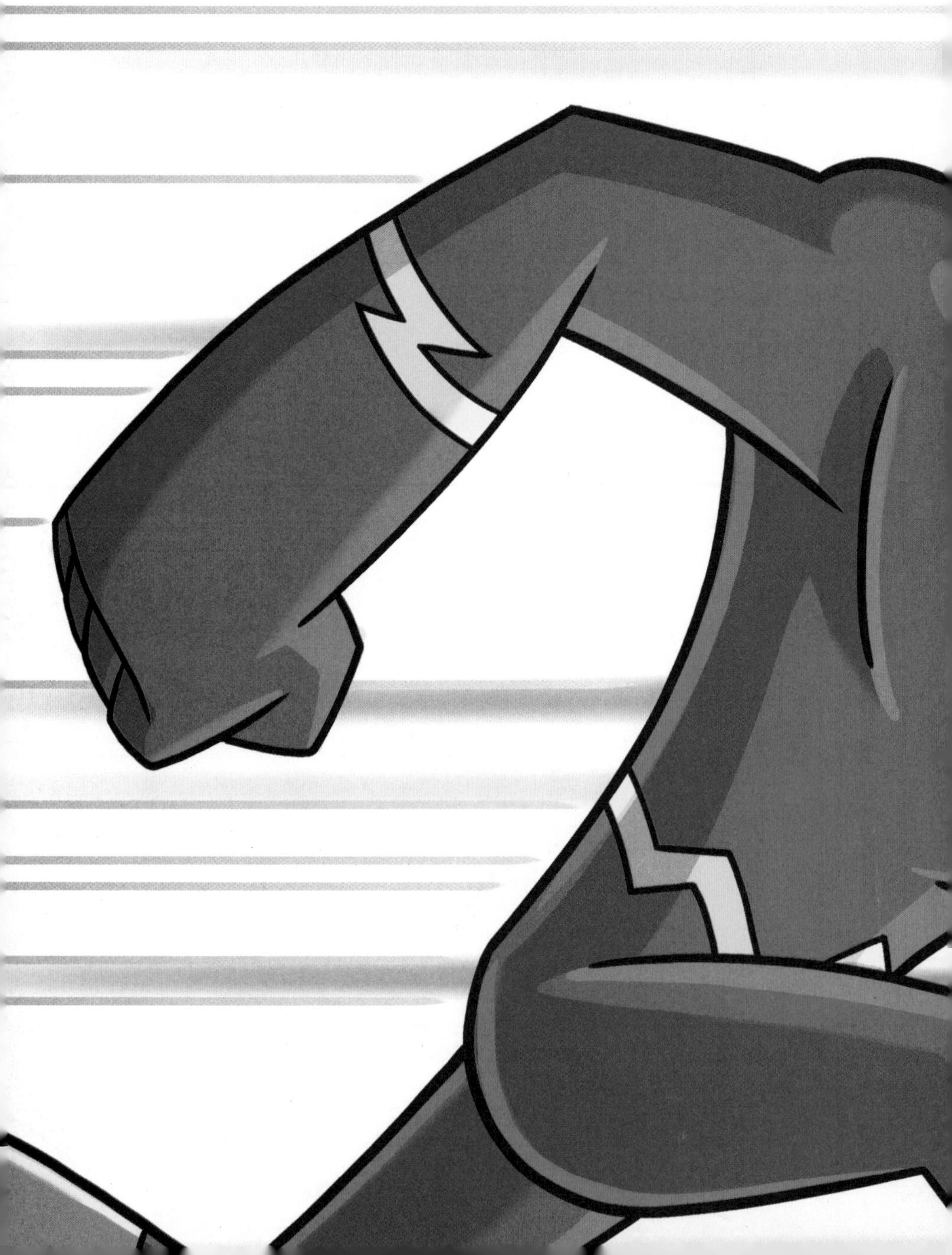

He became The Flash!

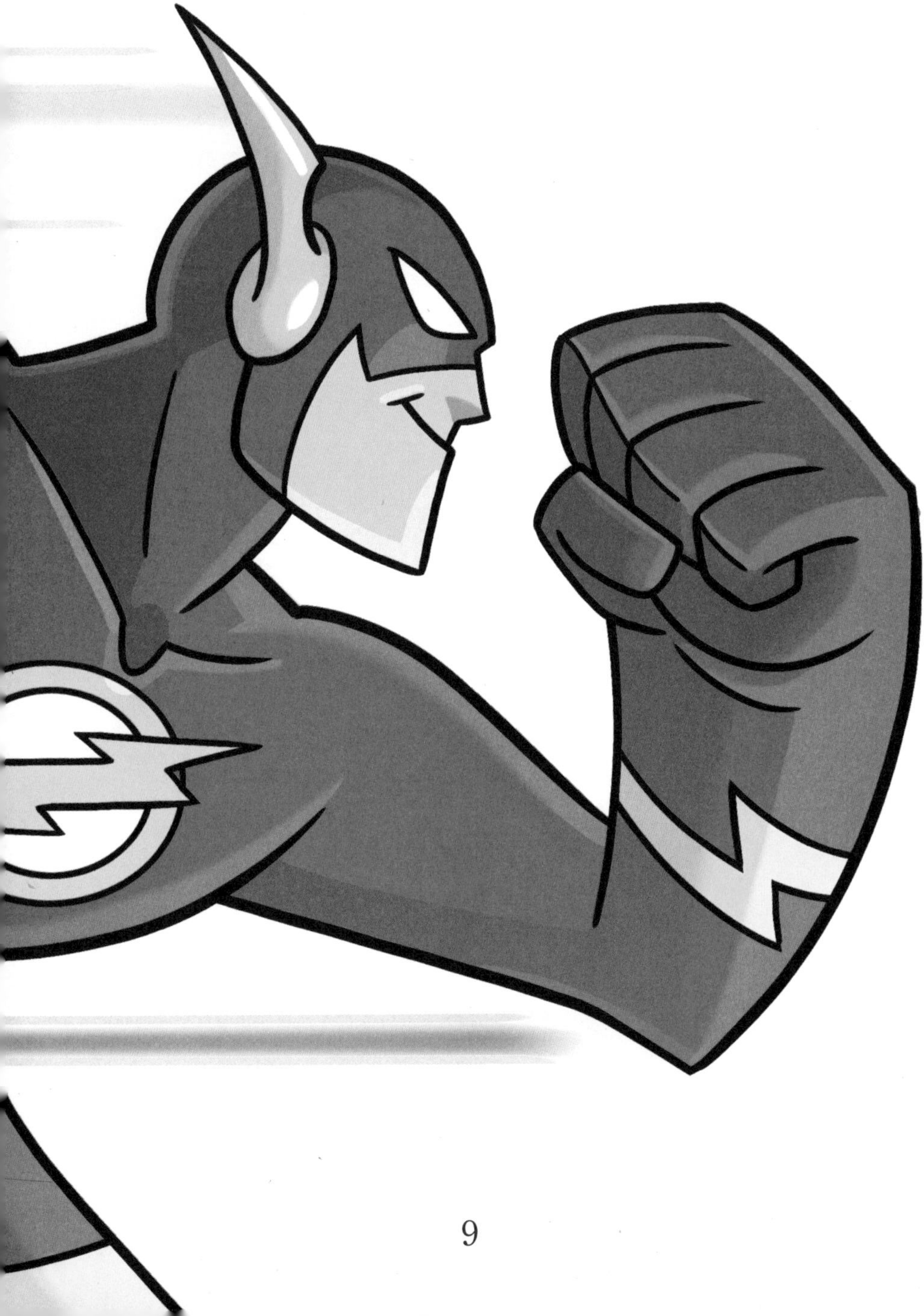

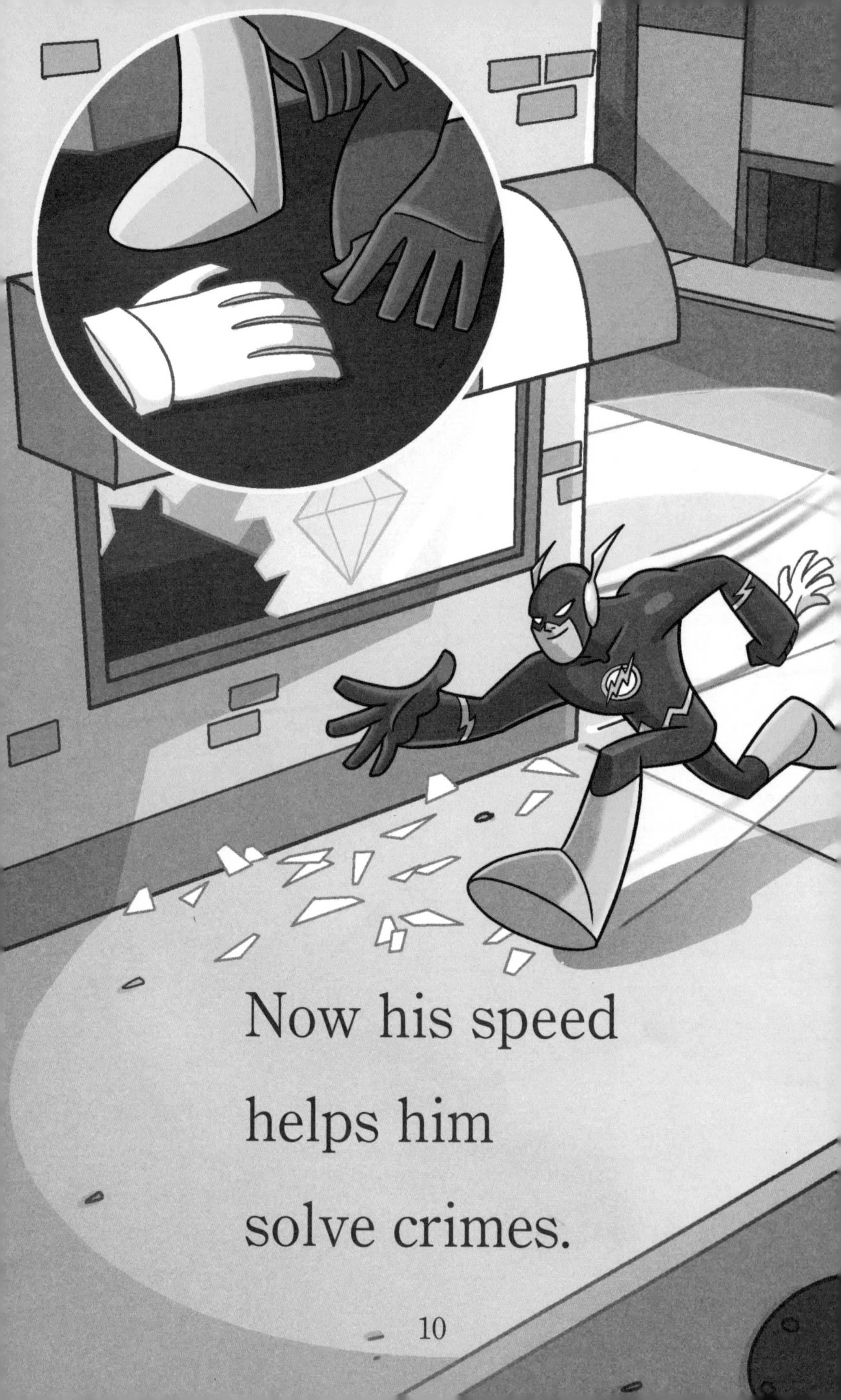

Now his speed
helps him
solve crimes.

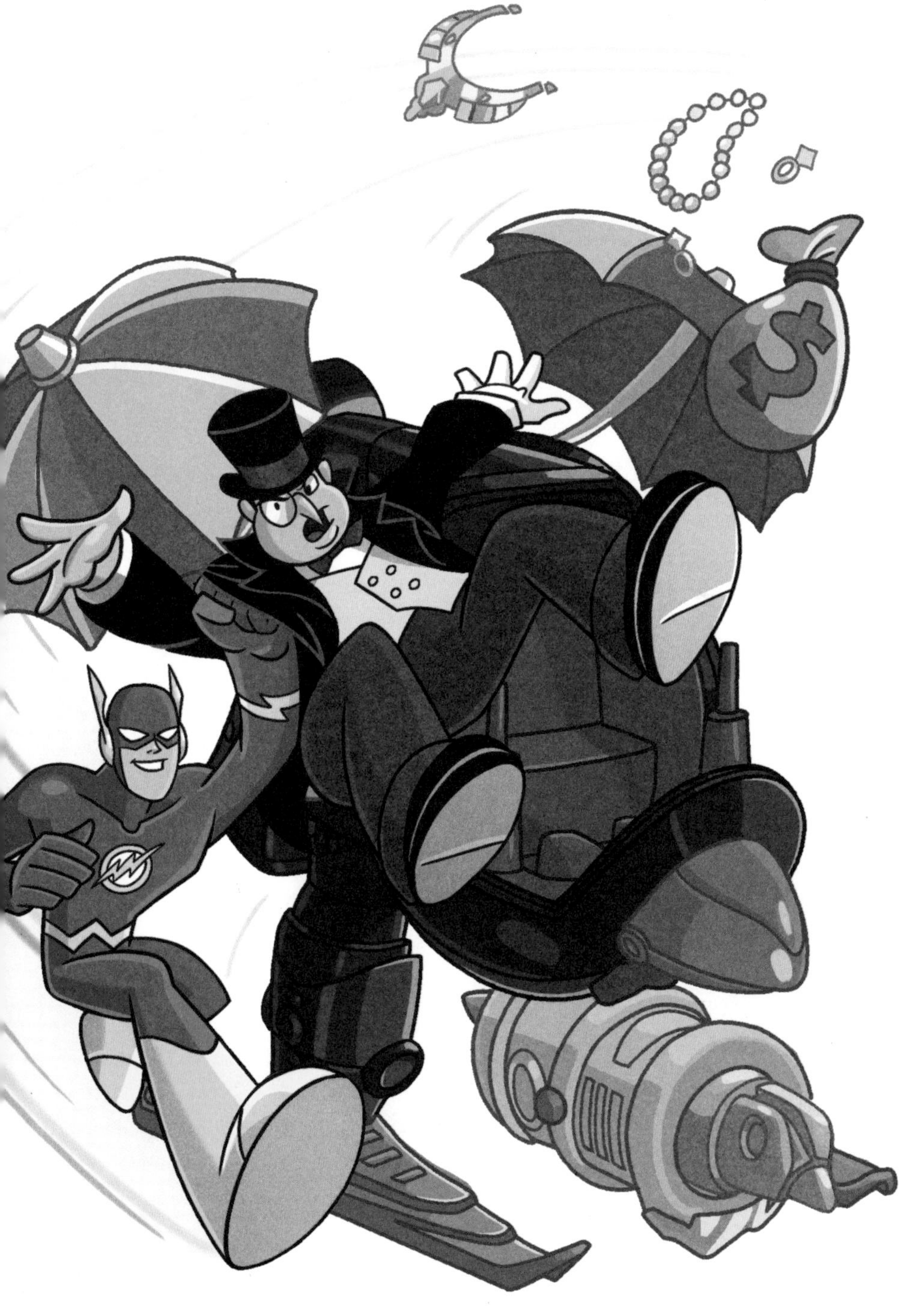

The Flash can run up buildings.

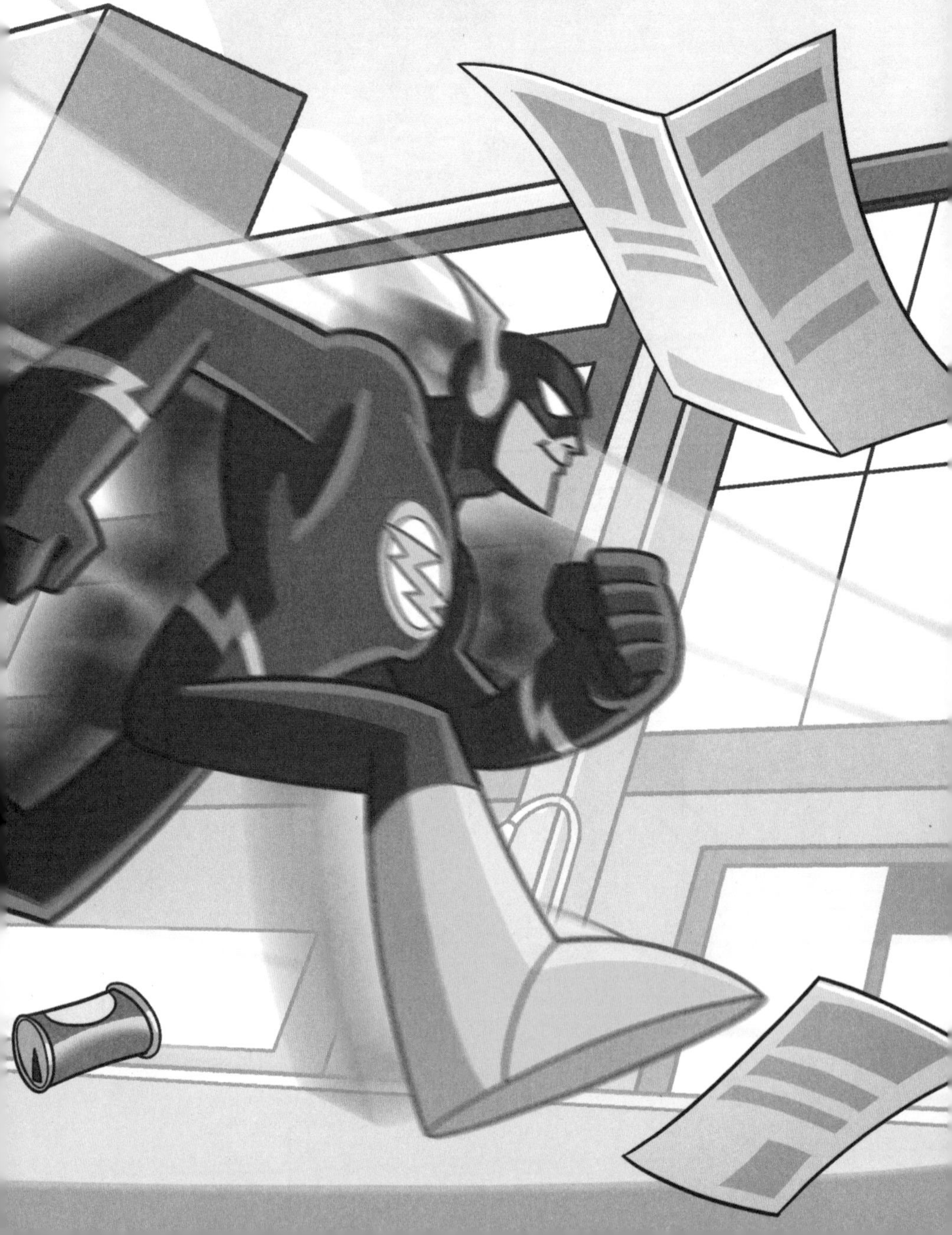

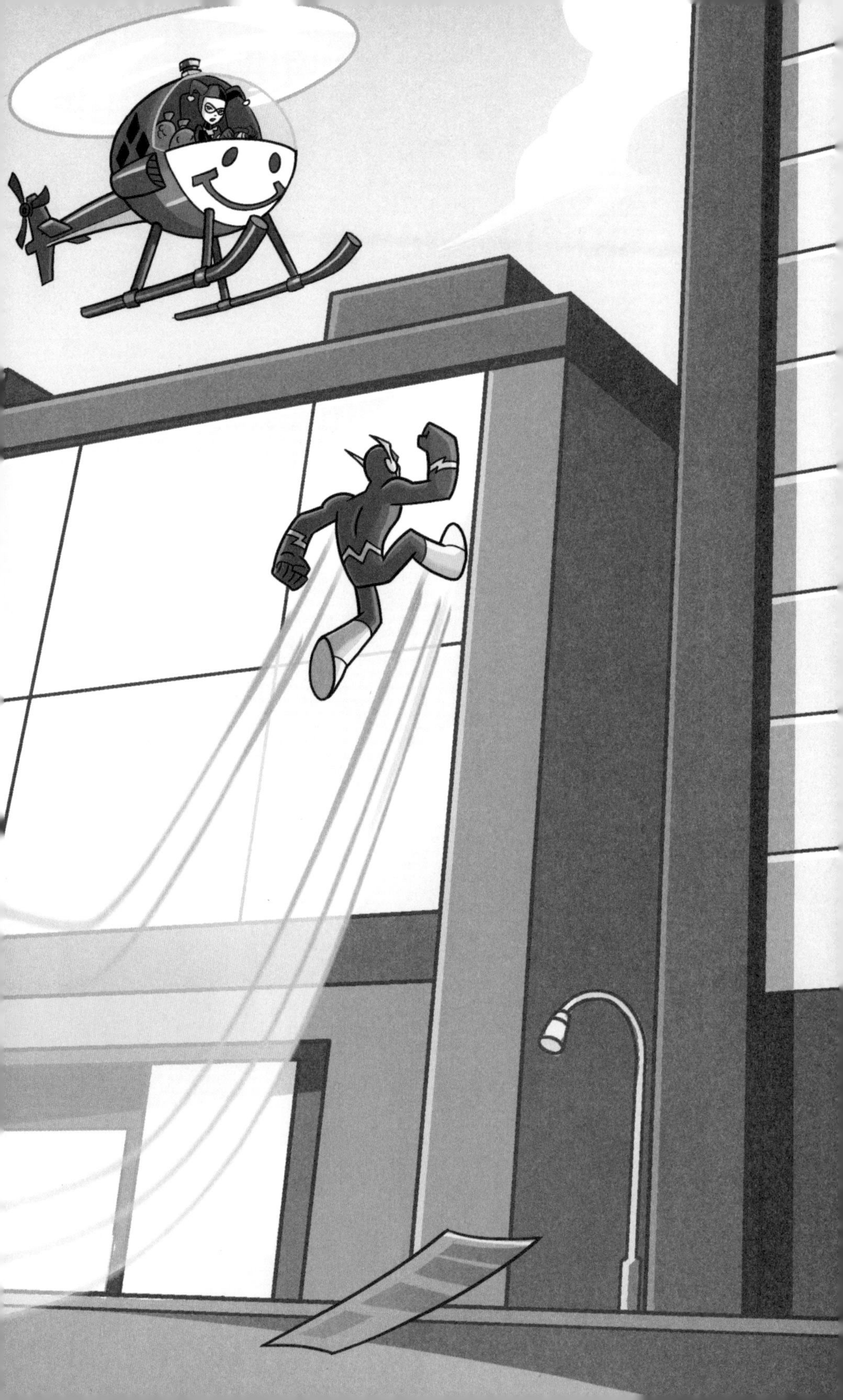

He can run
across the ocean
and create whirlpools.

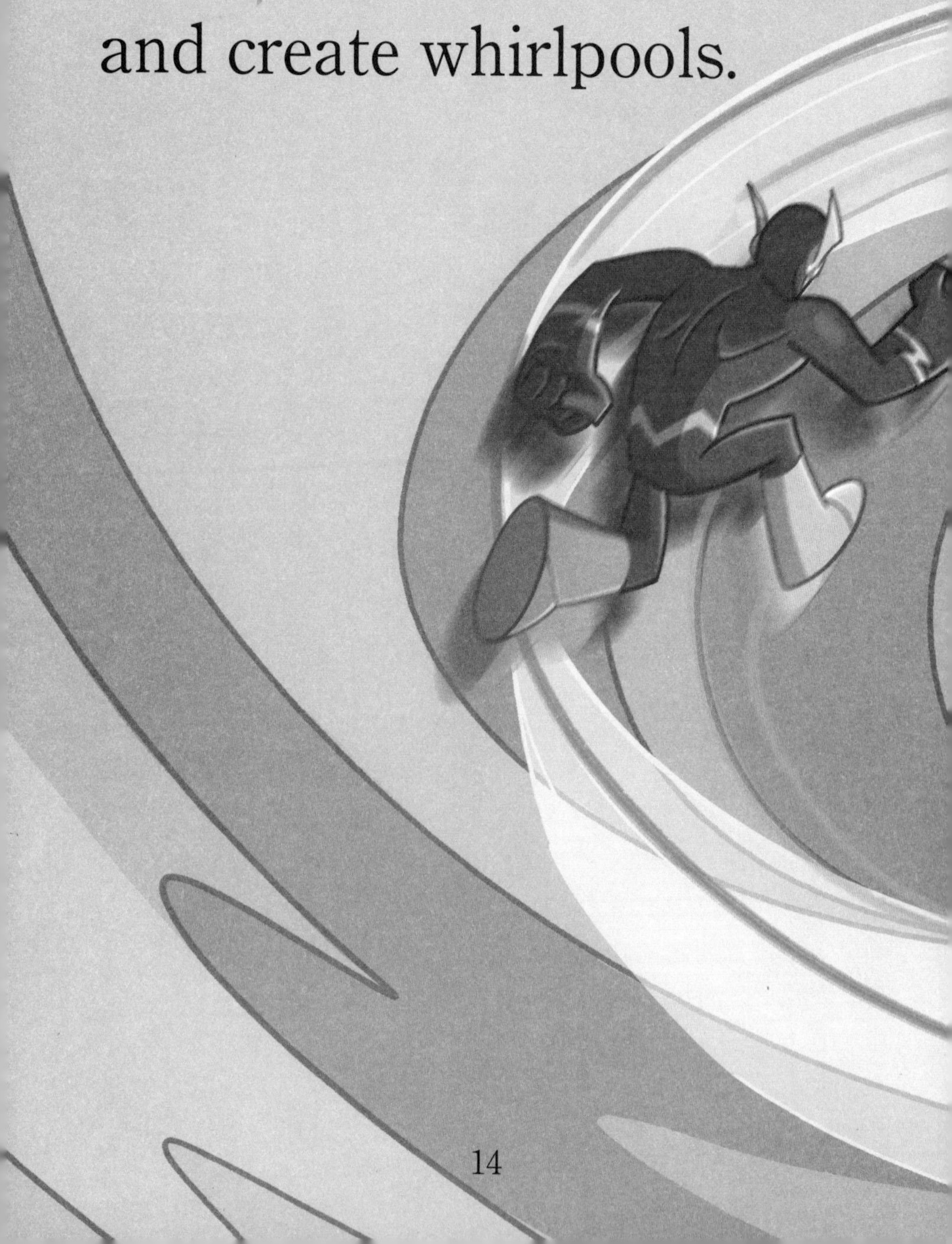

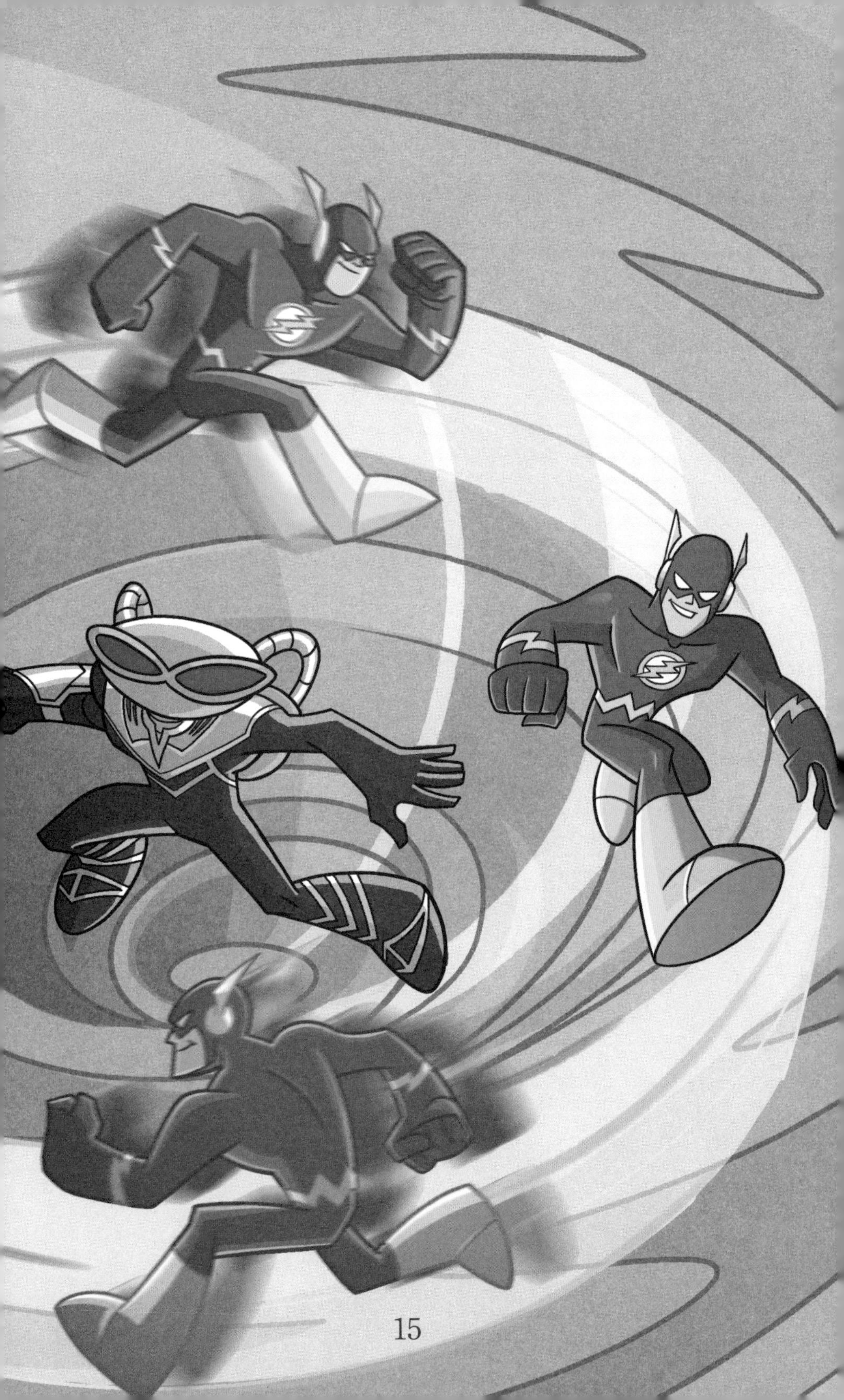

He can even run
around the world!

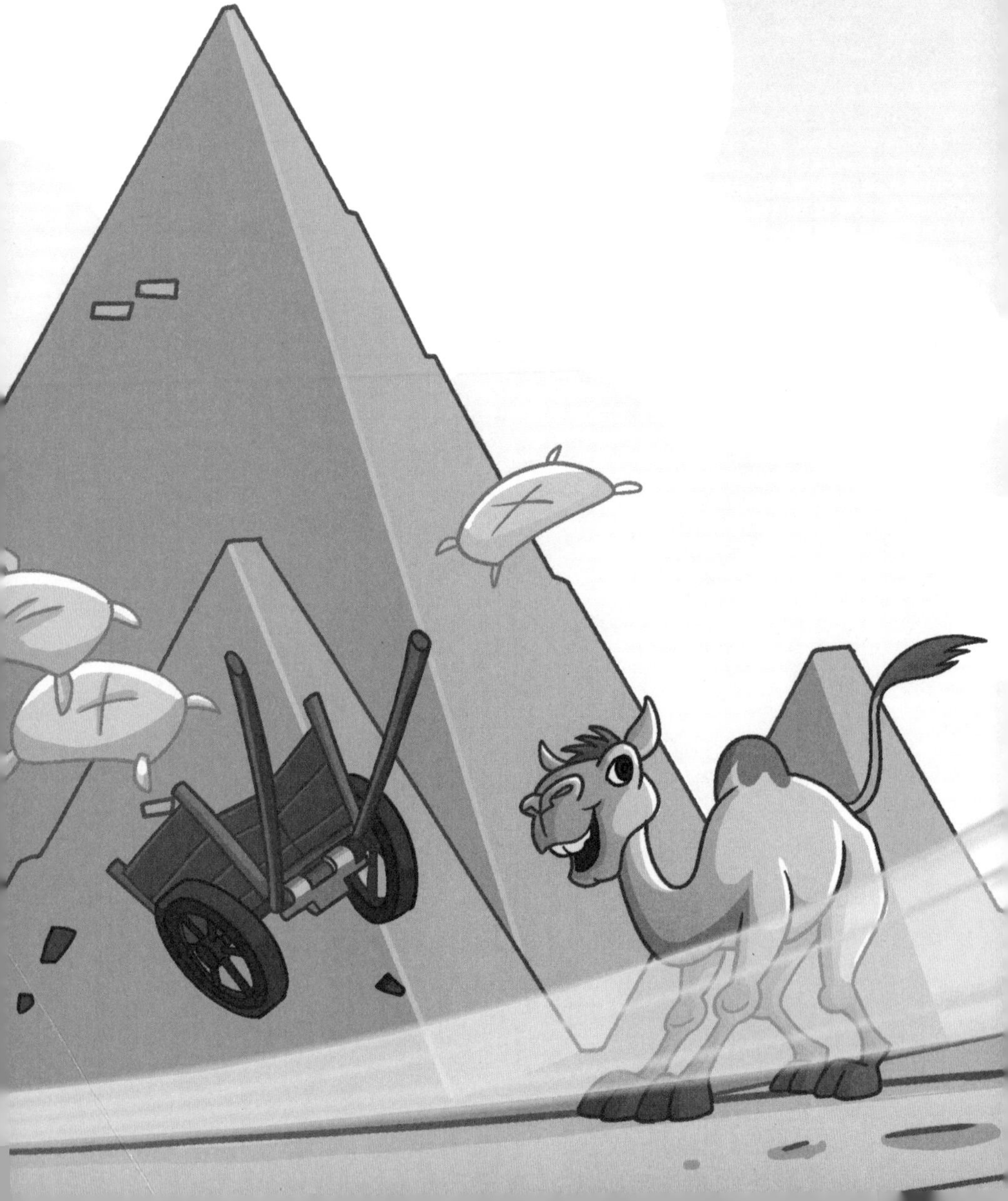

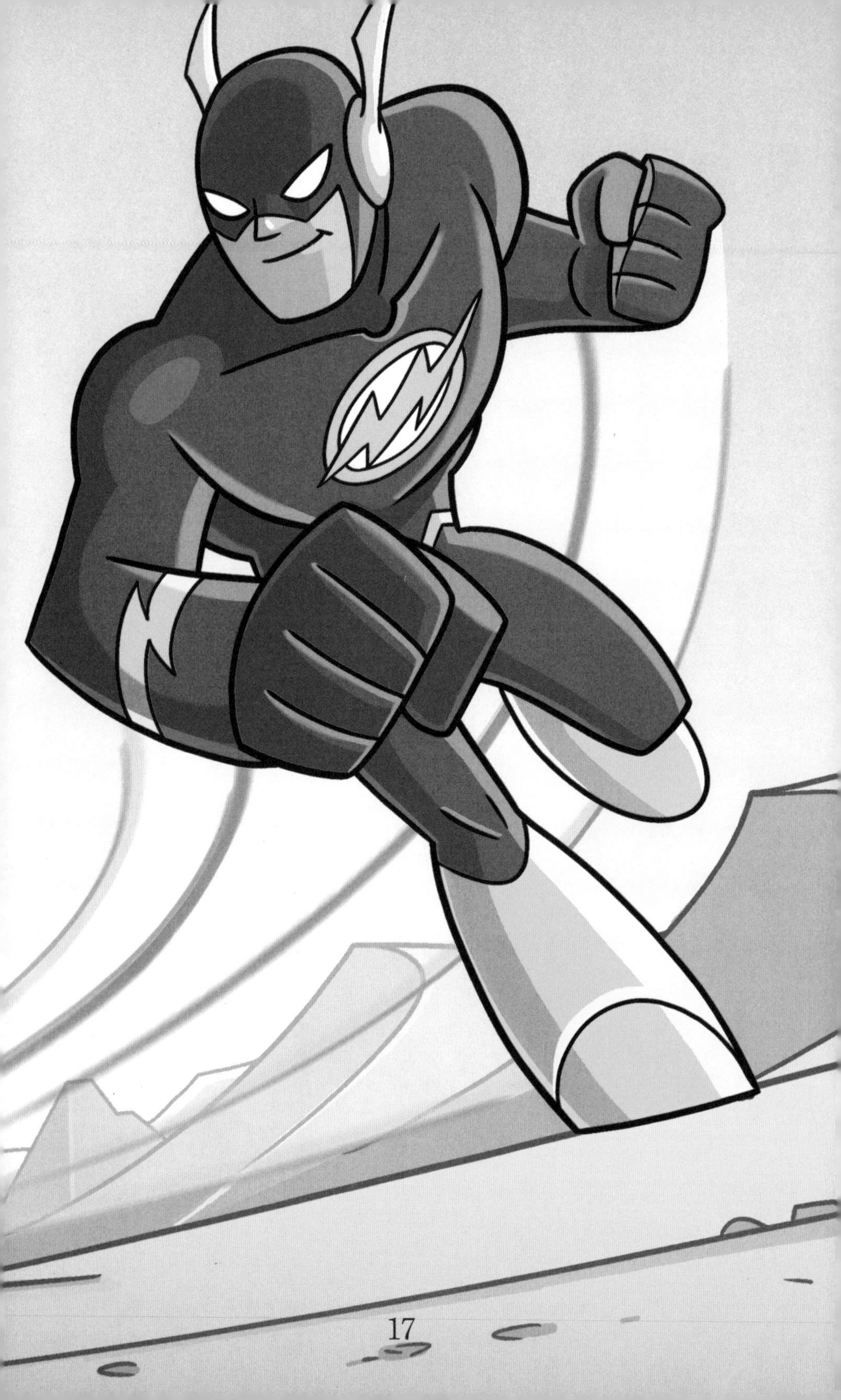

Cheetah is fast.

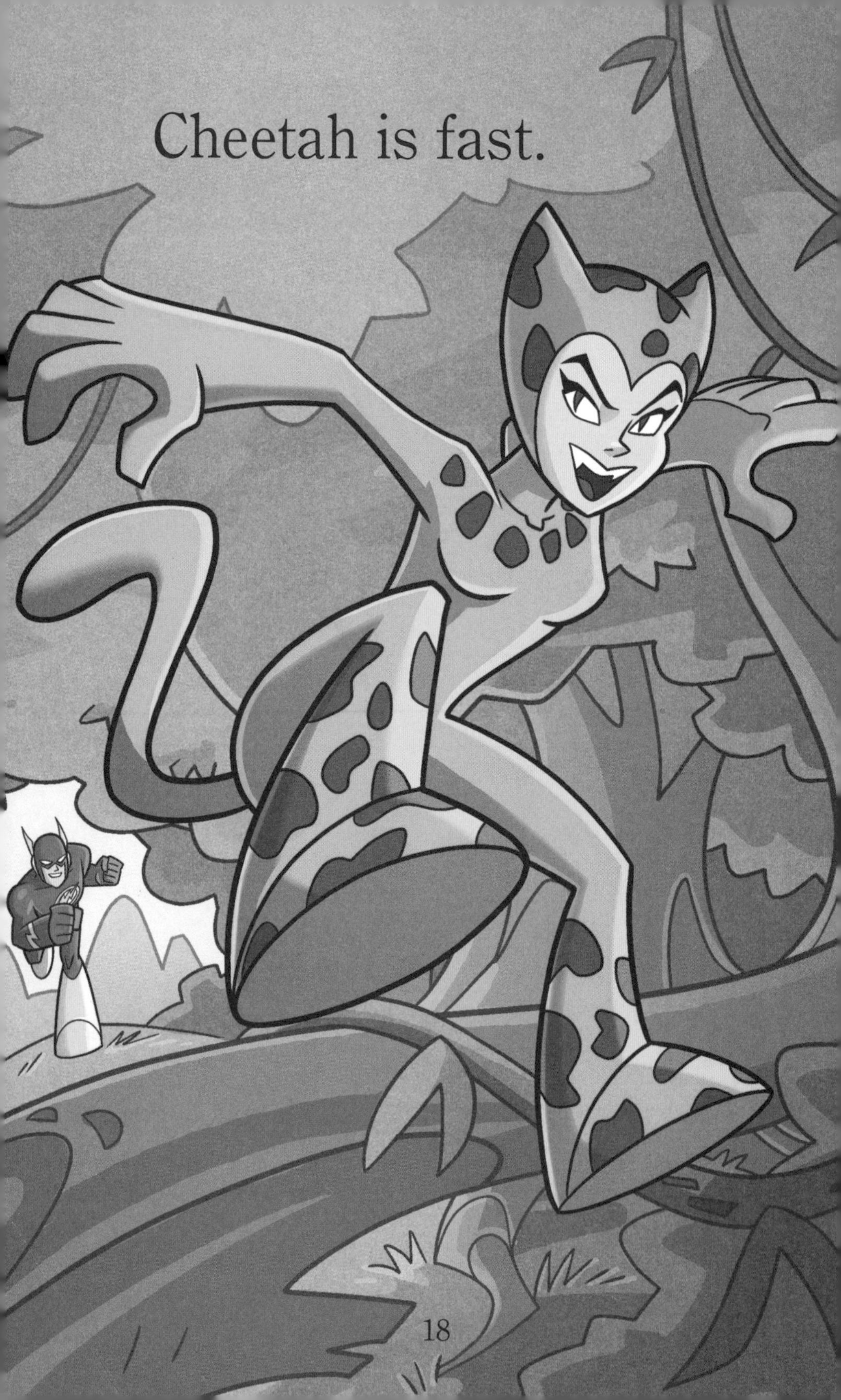

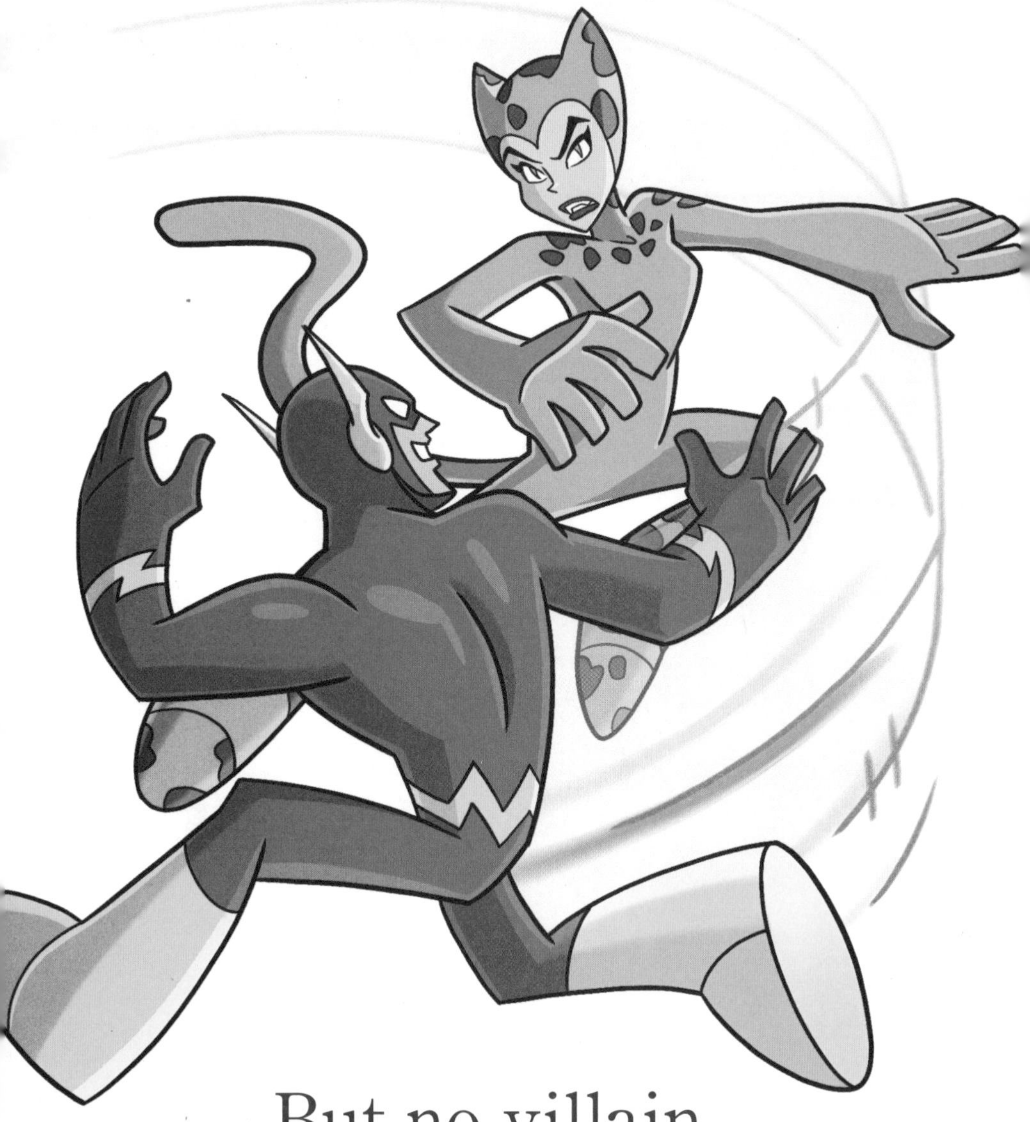

But no villain

can outrace

The Flash!

The Flash gets crooks to jail quickly.

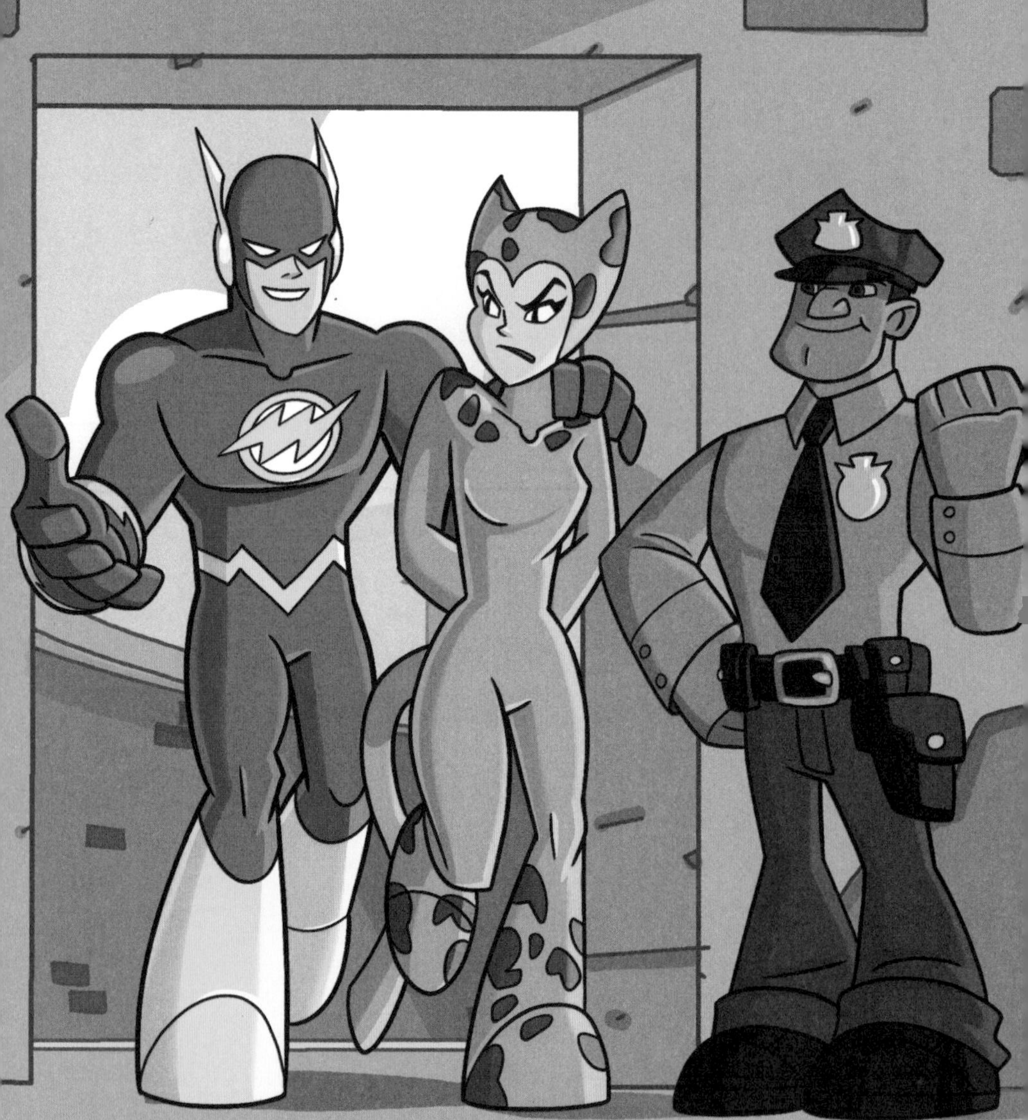

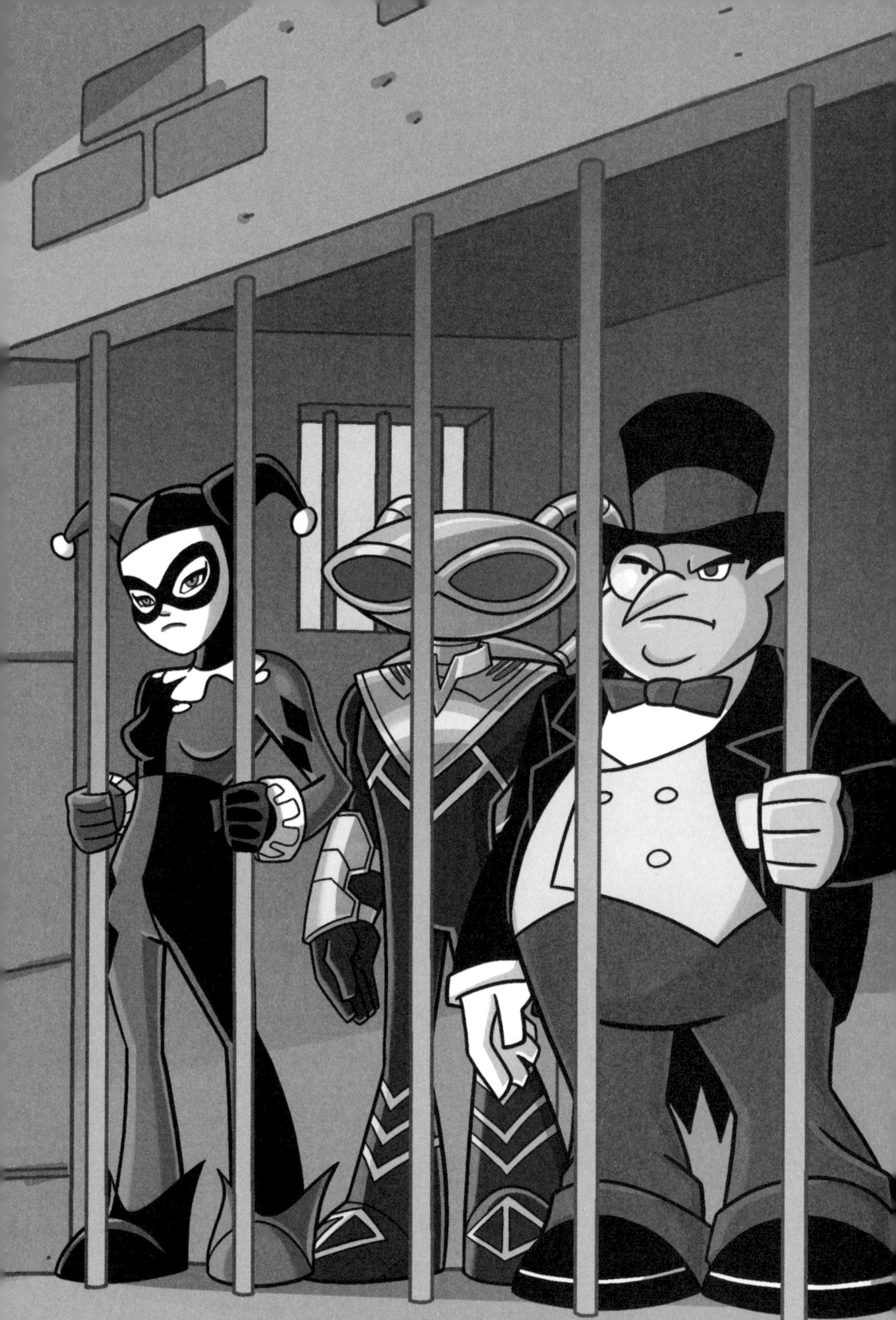

Who is as fast
as The Flash?

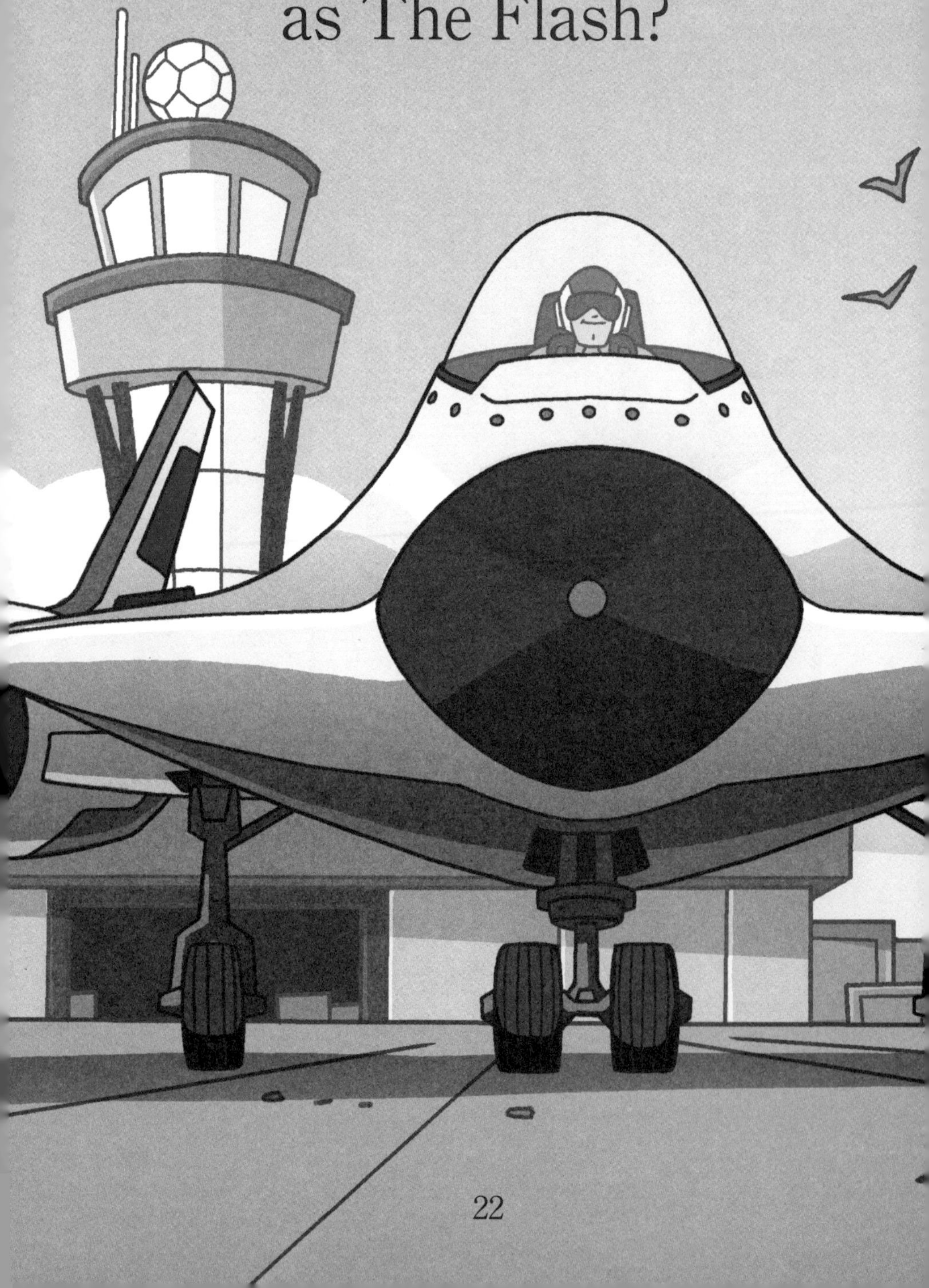

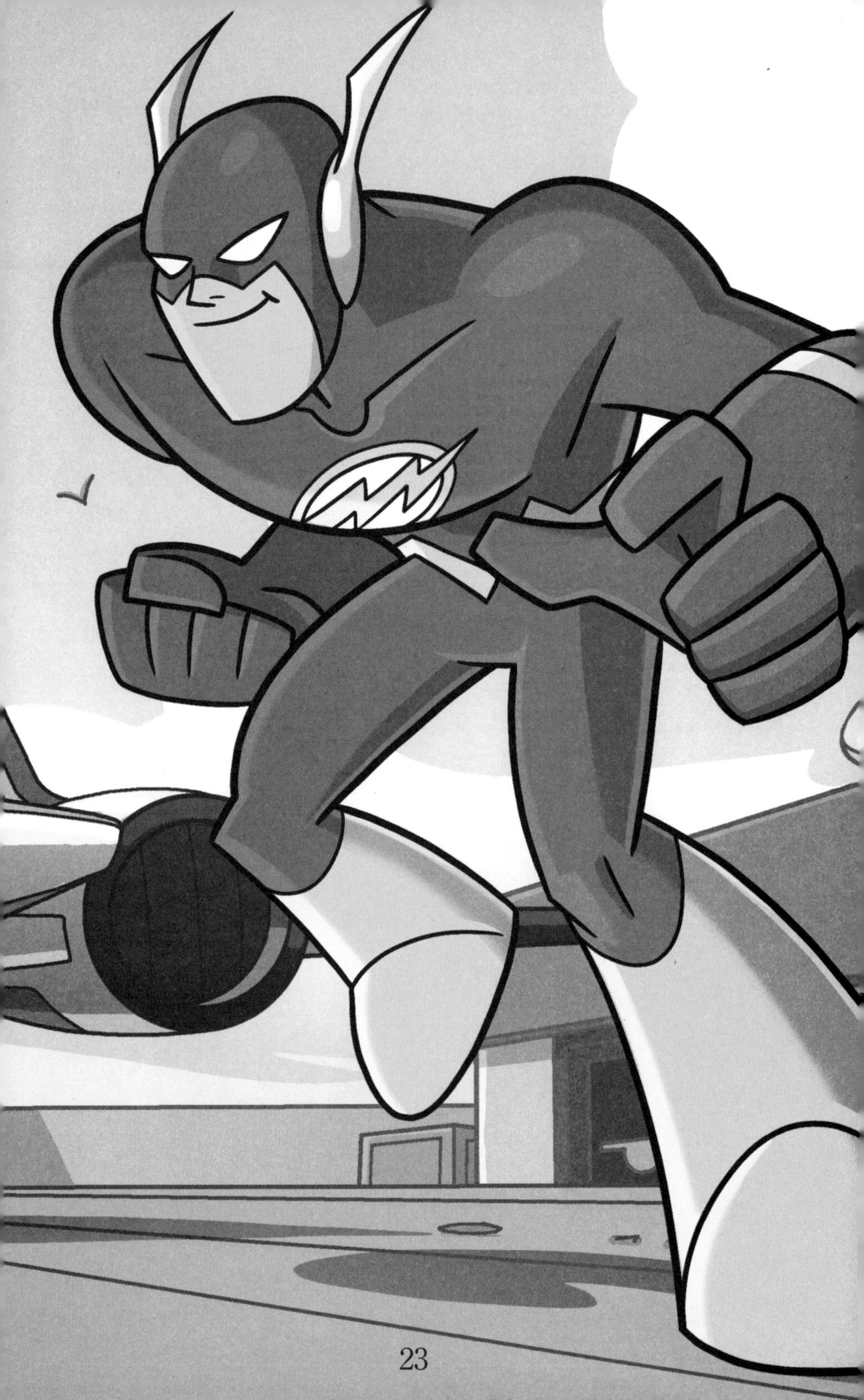

No one is as fast
as The Flash!

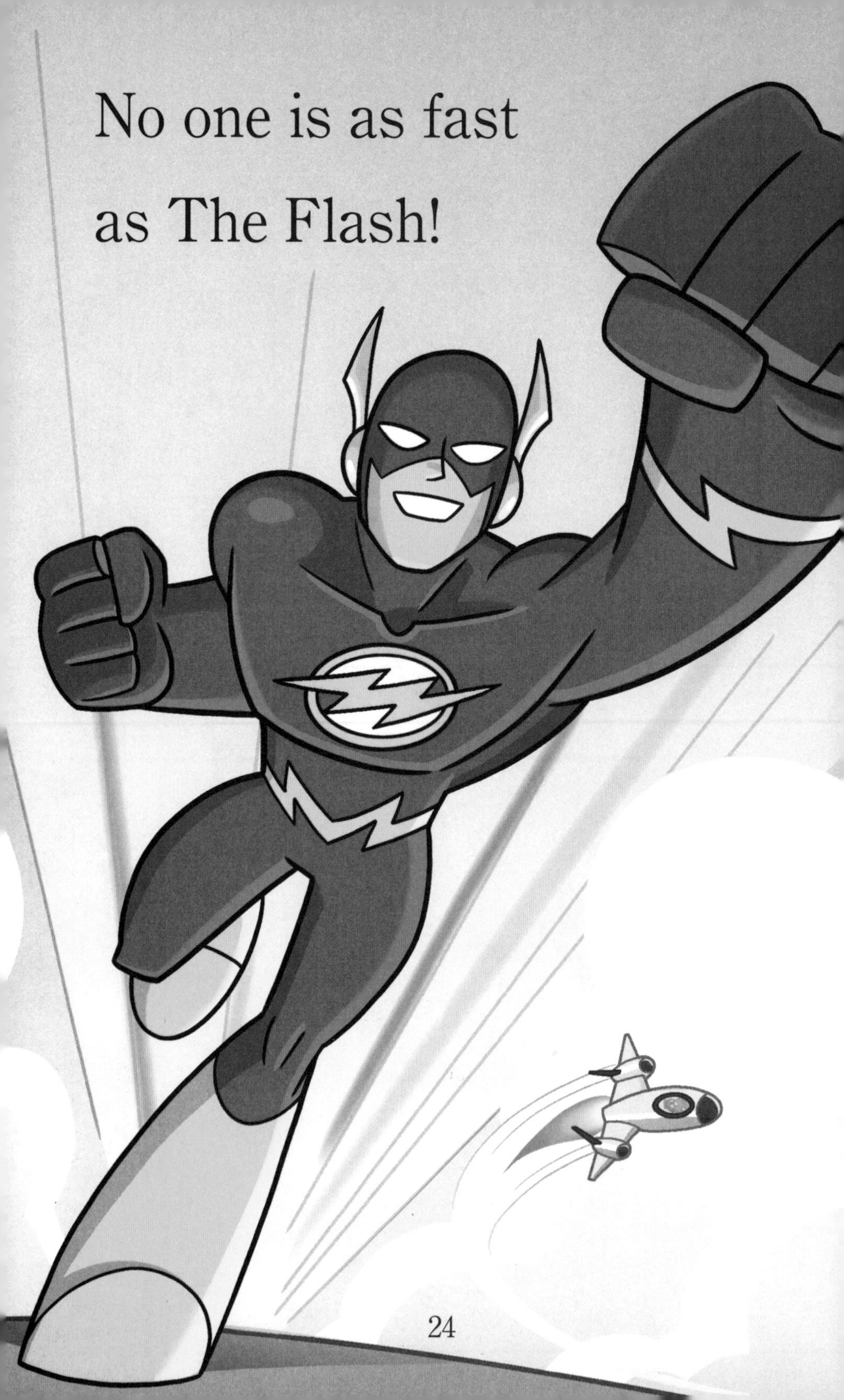